The Great Santa Stakeout

written by **BETSY BIRD**

illustrated by **DAN SANTAT**

ARTHUR A. LEVINE BOOKS

AN IMPRINT OF SCHOLASTIC INC.

For Jack Bird, one smart,
slick spy guy —BB

For Alek and Kyle —DS

Text copyright © 2019 by Betsy Bird
Illustrations copyright © 2019 by Dan Santat

LIBRARY OF CONGRESS CATALOGING-IN-PUBLICATION DATA AVAILABLE

ISBN 978-1-338-16998-0

10 9 8 7 6 5 4 3 2 1   19 20 21 22 23

Printed in Malaysia   108
First edition, September 2019

The text type was set in Futura Bold and Victorian Std.
The display type was set in Victorian Std.
The illustrations were created with ink, watercolor,
and Adobe Photoshop.

Art direction and book design by Marijka Kostiw

Freddy Melcher was Santa's #1 Fan.

He was the kind of kid who'd dress up
as **Santa** for birthday parties . . .

and Valentine's Day . . .

and even Talk Like a Pirate Day.

Freddy had **Santa** posters, **Santa** action figures, and **Santa** underwear. He was even saving up to buy his own pet reindeer. But there was one prize Freddy desperately wanted: a photograph taken *with* **Santa**, fresh out

Oh, it was risky. As every good kid knows, **Santa** only visits when everyone's in bed. It's awfully hard to sneak anything by someone who can see you when you're sleeping and knows when you're awake. That's why Freddy had to be extra good this year . . . at hiding his plans.

NORTH POLE

STEP 1 in Freddy's plan: String the roof with cans, so the sleigh can't land undetected.

STEP 2: Rig the whole living room with motion-sensitive cameras.

STEP 3: Put the milk and cookies on a pressure-sensitive plate.

STEP 4: Practice staying up late.

Finally, it was here. Christmas Eve.
No one suspected a thing.

Freddy was vigilant. It was almost midnight, and Ouita should be here any second, yeah . . . any . . . any . . .

CRASH!

What was that? The cans on the roof?
Freddy raced to the window just
in time to see . . .

DISASTER!

Something big rolled right off the roof.

Freddy tore outside. What had he done?

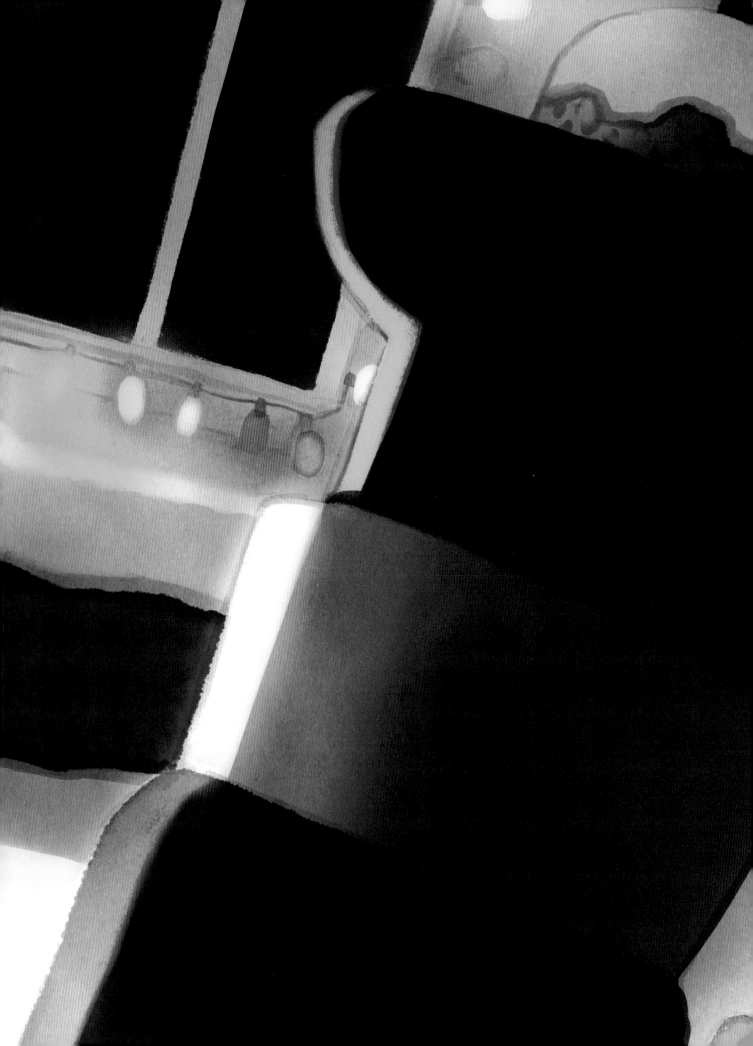

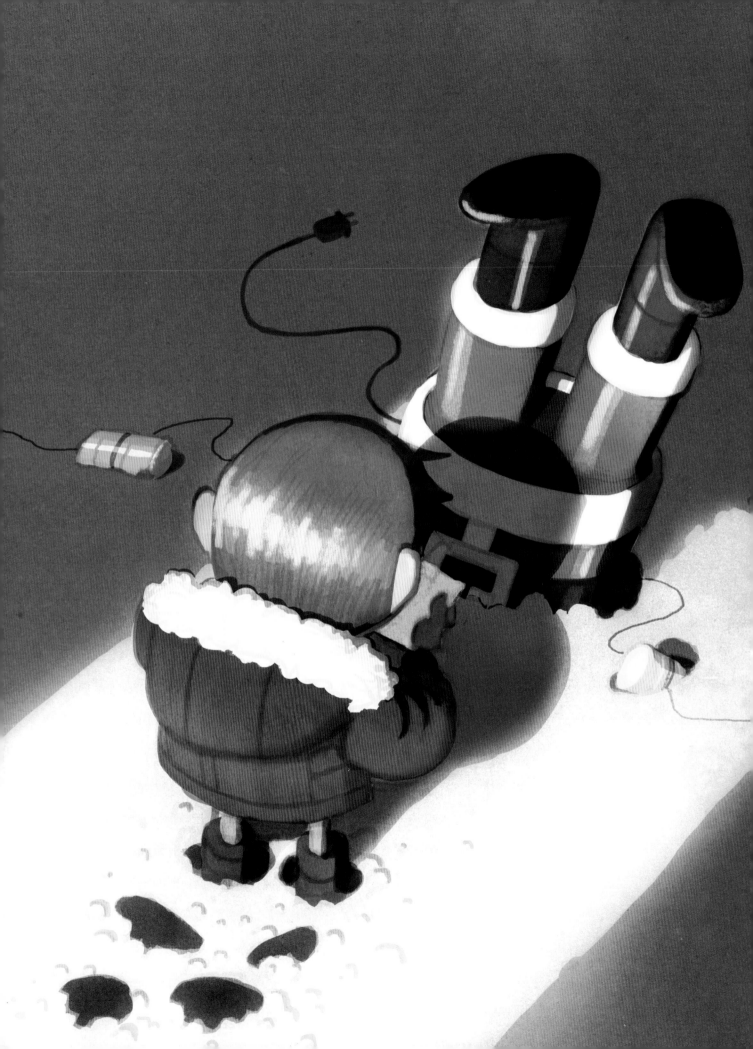

Santa had duped him and dashed!

Freddy was . . . angry?
No, that's not it.

Embarrassed?
No, no. Not that either.

He was sobbing his heart out,
pounding the snow,
having the most broken tantrum
of his short life?
Well, actually Freddy felt . . .

FANTASTIC.

While other kids nestled all snug in their beds, Freddy had played hide-and-seek with his hero! He even had a note from **Santa** that he could add to his collection.

So what if **Santa** got away this year?
It's fine. Maybe it's for the best.
Maybe no one can outwit **Santa Claus**...

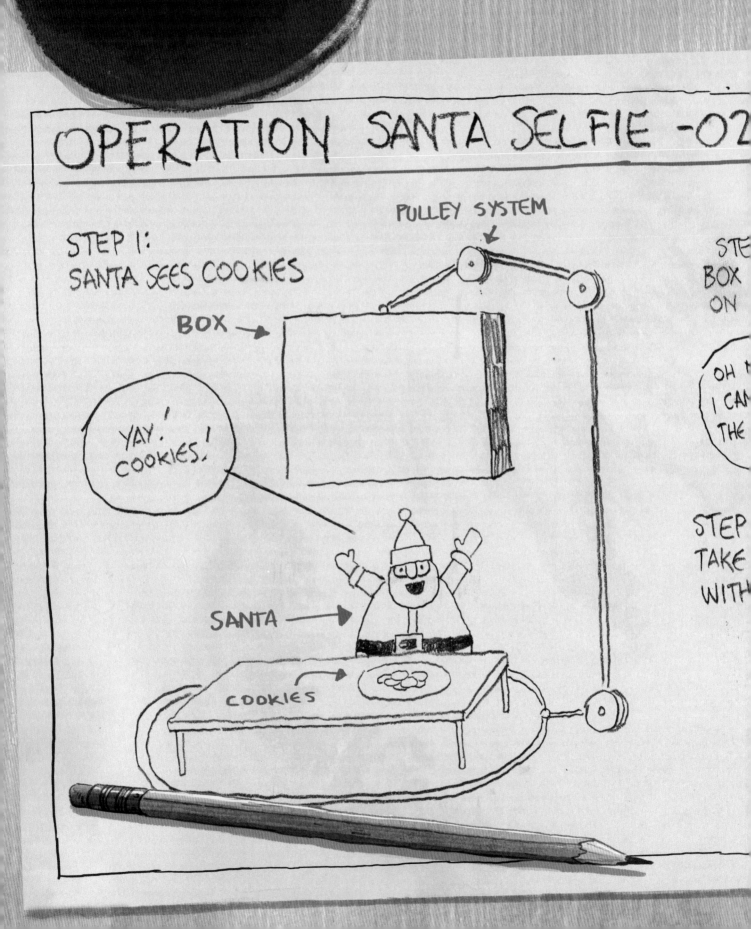